VIEWPOINTS AND PERSPECTIVES

VIEWPOINTS ON THE UNDERGROUND RAILROAD

★ PART OF THE PERSPECTIVES LIBRARY ★

KRISTIN J. RUSSO

Published in the United States of America by Cherry Lake Publishing
Ann Arbor, Michigan
www.cherrylakepublishing.com

Reading Adviser: Marla Conn MS, Ed., Literacy specialist, Read-Ability, Inc.

Photo Credits: ©Wikimedia, cover (left), cover (middle), cover (right); ©Wikimedia, 1 (left), 1 (middle), 1 (right); ©Wikimedia, 4; ©Wikimedia, 7; ©Everett Historical/ Shutterstock, 9; ©Wikimedia, 11; ©Wikimedia, 12; ©Wikimedia, 15; ©Picture History/Newscom, 16; ©Wikimedia, 18; ©Charles Nicholas/ The Commercial Appeal/ZUMAPRESS.com/Newscom, 19; ©meunierd/Shutterstock, 20; ©JT Vintage/ Glasshouse Images/Newscom, 21; ©Frilet Patrick/Hemis/ZUMAPRESS.com/Newscom, 22; ©Timothy O'Sullivan/Newscom, 25; ©Getty Images, 27; ©Getty Images, 29; ©Everett Collection/Newscom, 30; ©Wikimedia, 32; ©Everett Historical/Shutterstock, 35; ©Everett Historical/Shutterstock, 36; ©Everett Collection/Newscom, 38; ©Everett Collection/Newscom, 41; ©Everett Collection/Newscom, 43; ©Wikimedia, 44; ©Wikimedia, 45 (left); ©LOC/Newscom, 45 (right)

Library of Congress Cataloging-in-Publication Data has been filed and is available at catalog.loc.gov

Cherry Lake Publishing would like to acknowledge the work of The Partnership for 21st Century Learning.
Please visit *www.p21.org* for more information.

Printed in the United States of America
Corporate Graphics

TABLE OF CONTENTS

In this book, you will read about the Underground Railroad from three perspectives. Each perspective is based on real things that happened to real people who experienced or were linked to the Underground Railroad. As you'll see, the same event can look different depending on one's point of view.

1

HARRIET TUBMAN

UNDERGROUND RAILROAD "CONDUCTOR"

My name is Harriet, but they call me Moses. I know it is meant to be a compliment. Moses is a man from the Bible who led his own people, the Israelites, out of Egypt where they were enslaved, to freedom. I know they mean to honor me with this name. It means they trust me to lead my own people from the southern states north to freedom. It should not have to be this way, though.

We should have our liberty without having to run from **bondage**. It is a basic human right. Can they not see that we are human?

I suffered, oh, how I suffered, when I lived as an enslaved person. My experiences left me with lifelong injuries. When I was 12 years old, I was hit in the head with an iron weight. From then on, I have suffered from headaches and seizures and have had a difficult time falling and staying asleep. An enslaved person lives an inhumane life, and my mission is to help free all those who suffer as I have.

I was born Araminta Ross, but I named myself after my mother, Harriet. When I married, I took my husband's name, Tubman. The law says slaves are not allowed to marry, but I did so anyway. Most laws are not meant to benefit me. It is my right to be a wife. My husband's name is John, and I was proud to take his last name. He is a free man. The truth is, no matter what the law says, we are both free; we are all free.

I lost my husband because the law considers me a slave. I had to run from my home in Maryland in order to gain my liberty. John, who already had his freedom, would not come with me. I ran to Pennsylvania, where slavery is against the law. I wanted John to join me, but his life and livelihood were in Maryland. I could not change his mind. Still, I had to go. Slavery cost me my marriage. I would not let it steal my whole life.

THINK ABOUT IT

What is the main idea of this paragraph? Provide evidence to support your answer.

When I was a young woman, I took the Underground Railroad to Pennsylvania with my brothers. When I realized that I had crossed the Mason-Dixon Line and was on free soil, I remember looking at my hands to see if I was the same person now that I was free. I felt like I was in heaven.

The Underground Railroad is not a real railroad, although sometimes we do travel by train. It is a

DURING THE CIVIL WAR, THE MASON-DIXON LINE WAS CONSIDERED THE BORDER BETWEEN SOUTHERN STATES, WHERE SLAVERY WAS ALLOWED, AND THE NORTHERN STATES, WHERE SLAVERY HAD ENDED.

secret, or at least we try to keep it a secret. Some slaves are **tortured** into giving away information about this escape network, but we all do our best to keep information about conductors and helpers and fugitive runaways hush-hush. The work is dangerous, and I cannot do it alone. There are countless

HOW THE UNDERGROUND RAILROAD GOT ITS NAME

Several stories exist about how the Underground Railroad got its name. In one story, a slave owner feverishly chased a runaway slave all the way to the Ohio River. The fugitive swam across the river and crawled up on the other side. The slave owner watched in disbelief. He said it was as if he had disappeared on an "underground railroad."

SLAVE CATCHERS WERE PAID $10 IF THE PERSON WAS RETURNED TO BONDAGE AND ONLY $5 IF THE PERSON WAS FREED. MANY SLAVE CATCHERS LIED ABOUT A PERSON'S STATUS IN ORDER TO MAKE MORE MONEY.

conductors, like myself, and "station masters," who allow escapees into their homes or hideaways. If these good people are caught, the consequences are dire.

I'm thinking of a man, a hero, named Charles Torrey, who spent six years in prison for helping a slave family escape. Mr. Torrey is a well-known abolitionist, and our cause depends on the bravery of people like him.

There is also the story of Jonathan Walker. This brave sea captain was captured and arrested with a boat full of escapees whom he was attempting to bring to safety. Captain Walker was punished with a fine and imprisonment. Even worse, he was branded with the letters "SS." The letters meant he was a slave stealer.

These inhumane punishments do not stop us, however. If anything, they motivate us to push onward. We try to help as many runaway slaves as we can. We are most successful helping escapees from

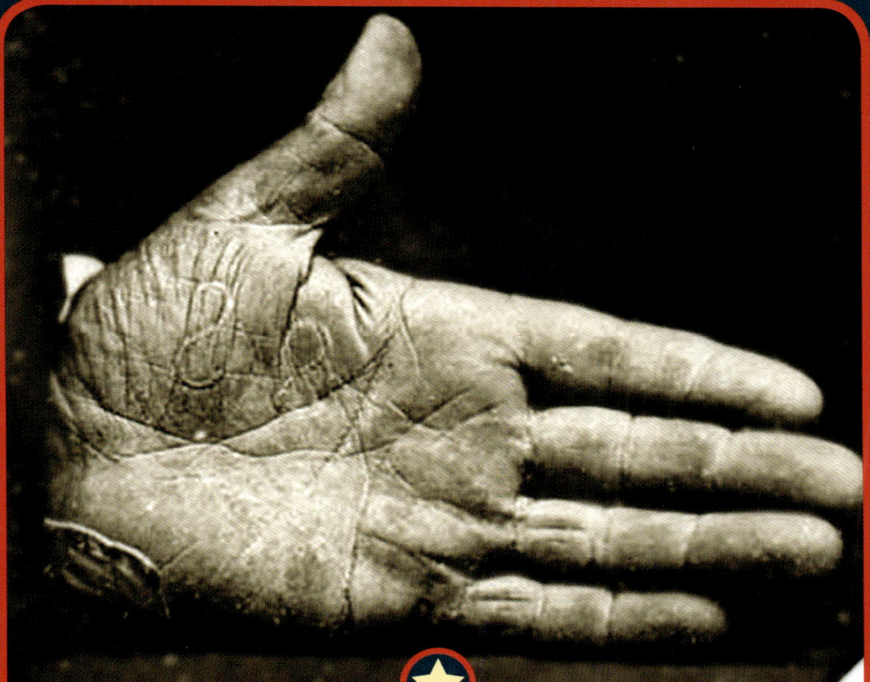

PEOPLE WHO INTERFERED WITH THE CAPTURE OF A RUNAWAY SLAVE WERE PUNISHED WITH HEAVY FINES, IMPRISONMENT, AND OTHER INHUMANE PUNISHMENTS, SUCH AS BRANDING.

border states, such as my home in Maryland. Maryland borders Pennsylvania, a **free state**. Slaves running from Kentucky and Virginia have only one border to cross until they enter free states, as well. Having to cross hostile territory through many slave

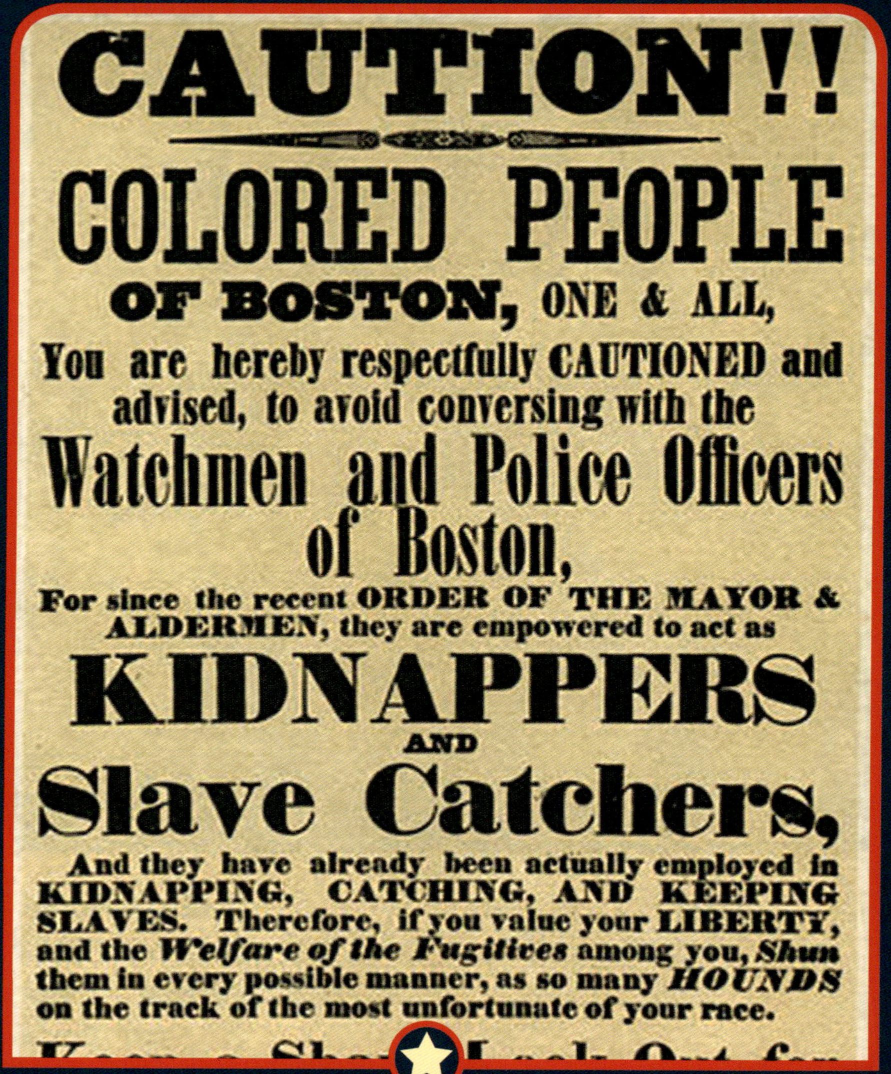

CAUTION!!

COLORED PEOPLE

OF BOSTON, ONE & ALL,

You are hereby respectfully CAUTIONED and advised, to avoid conversing with the

Watchmen and Police Officers of Boston,

For since the recent ORDER OF THE MAYOR & ALDERMEN, they are empowered to act as

KIDNAPPERS

AND

Slave Catchers,

And they have already been actually employed in KIDNAPPING, CATCHING, AND KEEPING SLAVES. Therefore, if you value your LIBERTY, and the *Welfare of the Fugitives* among you, *Shun* them in every possible manner, as so many *HOUNDS* on the track of the most unfortunate of your race.

IN BOSTON, ABOLITIONISTS STORMED A COURTHOUSE IN AN ATTEMPT TO FREE A KIDNAPPED FORMER SLAVE NAMED ANTHONY BURNS. FEDERAL MARSHALS PREVENTED BURNS'S ESCAPE.

states makes it more difficult for fugitives to reach safety. But we keep trying. We keep trying.

Living in a free state no longer guarantees an escapee his or her freedom. Since the Fugitive Slave Act of 1850, even runaway slaves living in free states are not safe. This new law requires people who used to be able to help us to, instead, turn us in. If they do not, they face grave penalties and punishments. Anyone found guilty of helping us could be imprisoned or fined $1,000. This is an enormous sum, far beyond the means of most folks, even if they did have the heart to help us.

Regardless, I continue as a conductor on the Underground Railroad. Securing my own liberty was not enough for me. I have crossed the line back into slave states time and time again. At first, it was to save my own family. But that was not enough for me. I want to lead all who are in bondage to a life of liberty.

Sometimes escapees lose heart. I understand this,

because running away to a new life can be frightening. But I must be tough. I must not let them give up. The consequences for us all could be dire if an escapee turns back. If they are caught, they could be tortured into giving information about those who have helped them. This is a risk I cannot take. So, yes, I am harsh. I scare escapees who threaten to turn back with my gun. I point it at them and say, "You'll be free or die a slave!" This usually brings them to their senses.

> **SECOND SOURCE**
>
> Find another source that discusses what happened when a fugitive slave reached a stop on the Underground Railroad. How is it similar to the account described here? How is it different?

This sounds barbaric, I know, but there is beauty in what we do. We use music to communicate. Since everything must be so secretive, and it is so difficult to know who is trustworthy, we use songs to send messages. An enslaved person who wishes to be led to freedom will sing "Swing Low, Sweet Chariot," and we will try to find this person and bring help. When I am in the South and looking for escapees who need help, I will sing "Go Down Moses" so that people who need help can find me.

Thankfully, not all Northerners are following the new slave law. There is a community of Quakers in

MANY QUAKERS, INCLUDING LEVI COFFIN, GAVE SHELTER TO SLAVES TRYING TO ESCAPE ON THE UNDERGROUND RAILROAD.

JOHN PARKER HALE WAS WELL KNOWN AS AN ANTI-SLAVERY POLITICIAN. HE SERVED IN THE HOUSE OF REPRESENTATIVES, THE SENATE, AND, IN 1947 AND 1952, HE EVEN RAN FOR PRESIDENT.

Delaware that helps us. We also count upon a community of Quakers in Dover, New Hampshire, that provides safe houses until we can smuggle fugitives over the border into Canada. In fact, with the election of Senator John P. Hale of Dover to the U.S. Senate, we had hoped the abolition of slavery could be accomplished quickly. Hale is the first senator who is openly anti-slavery. He even ran for president on an anti-slavery platform, but did not win. And so, we continue to wait for justice to be legislated and rely on the kindness of the likes of Israel Varney and the Knowles family, and other Dover, New Hampshire, Quakers who support our cause.

My work continues, even as it grows more difficult. Crossing a border to a free state is no longer enough. When I am the leader of a group of runaways, I try to bring them all the way to Canada. That is the only way I can be sure they will be truly safe.

2

Major Benjamin Chaires

Verdura Plantation, Leon County, Florida

William Shakespeare said it best in *Henry IV*, "Uneasy lies the head that wears a crown." Running my plantation and keeping things in order are becoming nearly impossible, and yet all the pressure and all the blame lies on my shoulders.

There is much to do here, running this plantation, and no one seems to understand the difficulty in getting it all done in time to turn a profit. Plantations are not new, and I did not invent them, yet they are an efficient way to produce goods and

BEFORE THE CIVIL WAR, COTTON PRODUCED IN THE SOUTHERN UNITED STATES MADE UP 77 PERCENT OF THE COTTON PROCESSED IN BRITISH MILLS.

NOT ALL SLAVE QUARTERS HAD COMFORTABLE FURNISHINGS OR EVEN FLOORS. MANY HAD DIRT FLOORS ONLY.

stimulate the economy. Any good businessman would see that.

It is not like during my grandfather's day, when it took all day to ready only 1 pound (.45 kilograms) of cotton for shipment. Everything moves so much more quickly now. Thanks to Eli Whitney's cotton gin, we can produce up to 1,000 pounds (450 kg) of cotton in only one day. It is a never-ending circle. Once I meet one shipping deadline, another looms! The more cotton we ship, the more they want!

ELI WHITNEY INVENTED THE COTTON GIN. IT WAS A MACHINE THAT WOULD SEPARATE COTTON FROM ITS SEED VERY QUICKLY.

AFTER THE INVENTION OF THE COTTON GIN, COTTON BECAME EVEN MORE PROFITABLE. THE DEMAND FOR LAND TO GROW COTTON AND SLAVE LABOR INCREASED. THERE WERE SIX SLAVE STATES IN 1790. IN 1860, THERE WERE 15.

I'm talking of both Great Britain and the northern states, of course. Mills in Great Britain, which **abolished** slavery decades ago, would be lost without our cotton shipments. And the North! Their self-righteous objections to the use of slave labor are ridiculous. The likes of John Greenleaf Whittier and William Lloyd Garrison—who complain relentlessly that our way of life is barbaric, inhuman even—do so most likely wearing southern cotton processed in northern mills.

ANALYZE THIS

In another chapter, find a place that discusses slavery's purpose and meaning. How are the two viewpoints alike? How are they different?

The South exports more than 1 million tons (.9 million metric tons) of cotton each year, much of it to Great Britain, but an enormous amount to the northern states as well. Hundreds of **textile** mills in Massachusetts and Rhode Island and all throughout New England demand cotton from the South. How are we expected to keep up with this demand if we employ wage-earning labor? The slavery system is the only system that will work. The slave system is what makes the United States the richest economy in the world, and the economic systems in the North and the South would crumble without it. The abolitionists should stop protesting and complaining. Their criticisms are unpatriotic.

There is an equally strong demand for tobacco produced by southern slave labor. It is time the abolitionists showed a little common sense. For one thing, their meddling only encourages our slaves to run away. This only causes trouble. When slave laborers run away, we must make an example of them, or we might have a **rebellion** on our hands. Punishing disobedient slaves is distasteful work, but it must be done. We employ the lash, of course, and other unpleasant methods. I do not like to get involved in that part of the business, so I leave it to my overseer. It is up to him to judge the severity of **infractions** and to

BETWEEN 1790 AND 1808, NEARLY 80,000 SLAVES WERE BROUGHT TO THE SOUTH TO WORK COTTON.

dole out punishments as necessary.

I prefer to cajole my labor force into working with incentives. Perhaps I will offer more food or other comfort items, such as blankets or clothing, to entice my slaves to work harder. This does not always work, but it is better when it does, so distasteful is the alternative.

And yet, they continue to run away. There has been a book published. It is extremely upsetting, and we generally do not allow its distribution in the South. It is Harriet Beecher Stowe's *Uncle Tom's Cabin*. This book is an outrage, quite frankly, and I tell you, it will lead to nothing but trouble. The Africans are not allowed to read, of course, but somehow some of them do, and they will be enticed to leave their posts by the promise of a better way of life up North. Irresponsible, but what can you expect from a woman novelist?

I do not understand why our slave workers run away, even with the influence of meddling

UNDER-PERFORMING SLAVE WORKERS WERE WHIPPED BY OVERSEERS AND FACED OTHER HARSH PUNISHMENTS. MANY SLAVES DIED FROM SEVERE INJURIES.

abolitionists. The southern slaves need one another, and they need us to watch over and care for them. Field hands are unskilled. They need the work of the slave **masons**, **coopers**, and metal workers to keep

THE RANKIN HOUSE

The Rankin House was built in 1825 and was home to Presbyterian minister John Rankin and his wife Jean. The couple were abolitionists and helped as many slaves as they could escape their lives of bondage. John Rankin once said, "My house has been the door of freedom to many human beings." He and Jean gave safe shelter to about 2,000 fugitive slaves. Today, the Rankin House in Ripley, Ohio, is a National Historic Landmark. Visitors can still climb the 100 steps from the river to the house.

LIFE IN BONDAGE WAS VERY DIFFICULT FOR SLAVE FAMILIES. OFTEN, FAMILY MEMBERS WOULD BE SOLD AND SEPARATED FROM ONE ANOTHER.

MANY SLAVE OWNERS BELIEVED THAT THEIR SLAVE WORKERS WERE INFERIOR AND COULD NOT SURVIVE WITHOUT THE SLAVERY SYSTEM. SOME SLAVE OWNERS EVEN ENCOURAGED FREE BLACK PEOPLE TO WILLINGLY BECOME SLAVES AS THEY BELIEVED THIS WAS THEIR "NATURAL PLACE" IN GOD'S DESIGN.

equipment in good condition. Slaves also provide such labor as cooks, nurses, and seamstresses would provide. Why pay for these skills if they already exist in the unpaid labor force?

Yes, sometimes force is necessary to keep things as they should be, but that is natural, and did not start with us, the southern plantation owners. This resistance to our rightful place as masters is becoming more and more difficult to handle. What most do not seem to understand is that it is only business, you see. It is nothing personal.

THINK ABOUT IT

What is the main idea of this chapter? In what ways do the main idea and details of the chapter surprise you?

HENRY BIBB

FUGITIVE SLAVE

I make no promise that my story will be easy to read. Remember, teaching an African slave to read or write is against the law, so I do not have a solid command of my letters. Nevertheless, I learned enough reading and writing to be able tell my own story. It is a hard story, but it is mine, and nothing can change that. If it can help another person who suffers in bondage, I think it is a story worth telling.

My mother told me that I was born in May 1815. The minute I was born, I became the property of her owner, David White, Esquire. According to my mother, my father's name was James Bibb, but he died before I could meet him. When the mistress of the plantation where we lived passed away, it was decided that the master's daughter be sent away to school. At that time, I too was sent away. My labors were rented out, and the money I earned was used to pay for the girl's education. I was only 10 years old. It was the first time I had been separated from my mother and my six little brothers. It was also the first time that I understood my position as a slave.

I did many different types of work for the owner of this new plantation. I worked in the fields in the worst kind of weather—rain and cold with my bare feet bleeding on the frozen ground. I have gone without food and without rest and without friendship or compassion for my tortured soul. Worse, I was punished constantly for mistakes I did not mean to make. I learned to run away into the woods to avoid the constant beatings.

Finally, I ran all the way home to the plantation where my mother lived. My original master, since he had remarried, allowed me to stay to serve his new wife. My job was to keep her rocking chair moving and to fan her to keep flies away from her in the heat. Oh, how I hated this demeaning "work." Soon, she got sick of me, and I was hired out again.

SECOND SOURCE

Find another source that describes the life of a passenger on the Underground Railroad. How does it compare and contrast to Henry Bibb's life?

Before long, I was again subject to unfair beatings. Floggings and whippings were constant, and I often suffered without enough food or rest. But the worst **deficiency** of all was my lack of knowledge. Slaves are not allowed to read books! They may not learn to read and write! They are kept in ignorance all

SLAVE WORKERS WHO WORKED INSIDE THE HOMES OF PLANTATION OWNERS OFTEN HAD BETTER LIVING CONDITIONS. THEY WERE CALLED DOMESTIC SLAVES AND WERE OFTEN GIVEN BETTER LIVING QUARTERS AND MORE FOOD.

of their lives. This, this I cannot accept! If I wish to improve my mind, I have no choice but to break the bonds of my enslavement. I will run away to the

North.

It will not be easy, this I know, for I have heard stories of what happens to escapees who are caught.

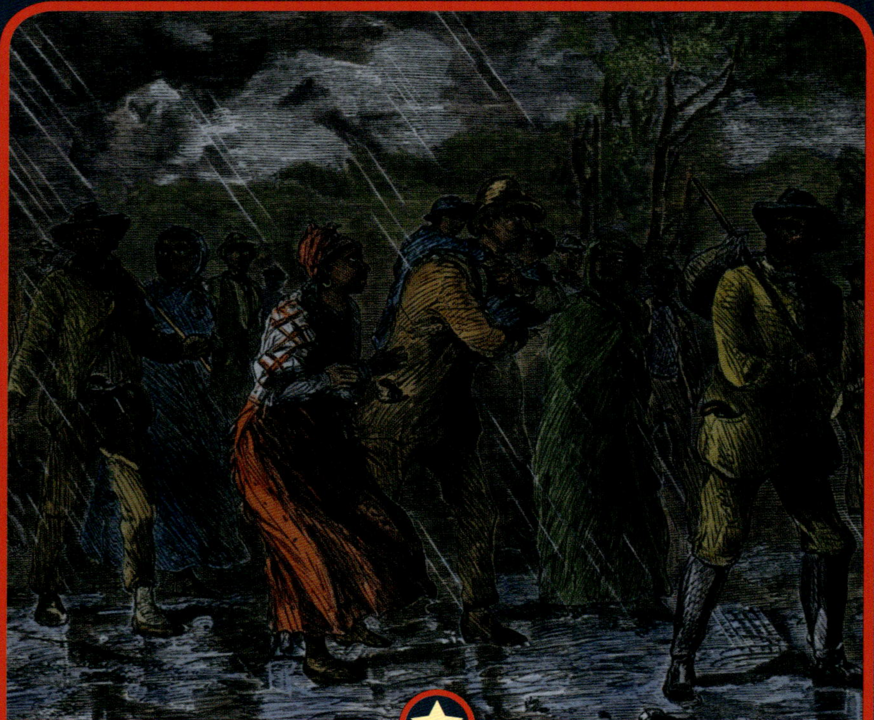

THERE WERE MANY WILLING UNDERGROUND RAILROAD CONDUCTORS IN THE CITY OF WILMINGTON, DELAWARE. FOR MANY FUGITIVE SLAVES, IT WAS THE FINAL STOP BEFORE THEY REACHED FREEDOM IN PHILADELPHIA AND NEW JERSEY.

They are beaten and whipped and tortured. To resist enslavement often means death to the slave. What do I have to lose? I know I have to run away.

ANALYZE THIS

Find another narrative that details the dangers of taking part in the Underground Railroad. How is it similar to or different from what you read here?

I made a plan. I would run into the woods. I would run all the way to Canada, where persons of color are considered real men and women, not livestock or **chattel**. I would not stop running until my freedom and liberty were assured. I made a choice that may seem odd to you, but one that I thought would protect me from detection. When I ran away, I took a horse's bridle with me. That way, if any one asked if I were a runaway, I could answer no, that I was simply looking for a runaway mare.

Another part of my decision may also be hard for you to understand. I left behind my wife, Malinda, and our young daughter. I could not tell her in advance that I planned to run to Canada, but I did send her a message that I would return for her. And I did, but not before completing my long and difficult journey to the North.

FUGITIVE HENRY BIBB RAN AWAY AND WAS RECAPTURED SEVERAL TIMES BEFORE HE ULTIMATELY ACHIEVED FREEDOM. HE TRIED TO REUNITE WITH HIS FAMILY, BUT THE SLAVERY SYSTEM KEPT HIM AWAY FROM HIS WIFE AND CHILD.

After crossing the Ohio River into Indiana, I knew I had to keep going. Indiana is a free state, but no man is free in a country where slavery is legal anywhere. I took a steamboat to Cincinnati, Ohio, and used the resources provided to me by the kind people along the Underground Railroad to reach Canada. I had only a little money and did not have much food on my journey. I never would have made it without help from the Underground Railroad. Kind friends were made known to me with secret signals, and they gave me food and shelter on my journey. There was one point where I was advised to stop at the home of a known abolitionist, a friend who supported my attempt to flee to liberty, but I was too afraid to stop. Slave catchers abounded, and with them their brutal hunting dogs. My journey on the Underground Railroad was one of both fear and gratitude.

Though I did not have the courage to stop at first, weariness soon overcame me, and I had no choice.

Luckily, there were safe places along the way where I could hide and rest for a short while. There were compassionate people who gave me food and told me

WILLIAM LLOYD GARRISON

William Lloyd Garrison was a famous abolitionist who worked for civil rights for enslaved African Americans through journalism. Born December 10, 1805 in Newburyport, Massachusetts, Garrison began an abolitionist journal called the *Liberator* in 1830. He also helped found an abolitionist group called the New England Anti-Slavery Society in 1832. This group invited fugitive slaves, such as Frederick Douglass, to speak and to recount their experiences as slave workers. Garrison died on May 24, 1879 in New York City.

where to go next for the safest route. Their help and advice helped me **elude** slave catchers, and I made it all the way to Canada! I was free! But I could not live without my wife and daughter. I found work and

BIBB WAS RECAPTURED SEVERAL TIMES ON HIS JOURNEY TO FREEDOM.

saved enough money to return for those that I loved. This was a mistake, but I could not help myself. I have a right to provide for and to be with my family. I only wanted to exercise that right.

I was captured on my return for Malinda and arrested. I vowed that my captivity would not last. For short spurts of time, I was allowed to be with my family. After the death of our youngest child, a frail daughter who was neglected by Malinda's owner, I knew I had to break free for good and forever. Our plans to escape as a family were never possible. After a time, Malinda lost faith and gave up that we would ever be free together. When I learned that she had left me and remarried, I made my final escape to Canada.

I return now and then to tell my story. If my story helps one man, woman, or child who is enslaved in the South, than the risk to reenter the United States to tell it will be worth it. It is my dream that one day, there will be "justice and liberty for all."

HENRY BIBB WROTE TO HIS FORMER "OWNER" AND SAID THAT THE BRUTAL TREATMENT OF HIS FAMILY WAS ONE OF MANY REASONS HE RAN AWAY. "MY INFANT CHILD WAS ALSO FREQUENTLY FLOGGED . . . " BIBB WROTE.

TIMELINE

UNDERGROUND RAILROAD

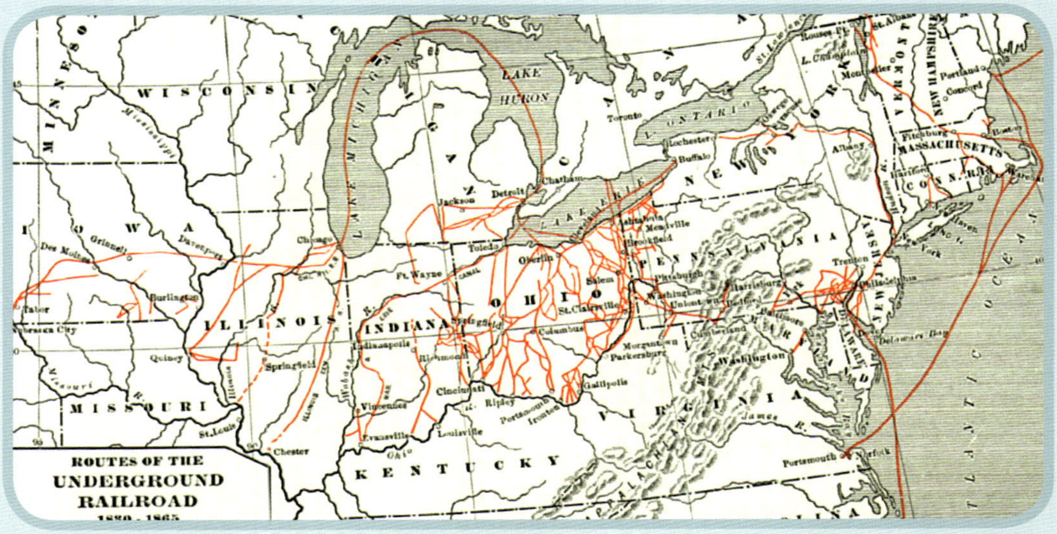

George Washington complains that one of his runaway slaves was aided by "a society of Quakers, formed for such purposes." This is considered the first mention of an already established Underground Railroad.

1786

Harriet Tubman is born Araminta Ross in Dorchester County, Maryland.

1819

White abolitionist neighbors help Tubman make her first escape to the North. This is her first time traveling the Underground Railroad.

1849

1810–1850

More than 100,000 fugitives escape enslavement using the Underground Railroad.

1850

Harriet Tubman officially becomes a "conductor" on the Underground Railroad. She returns to the southern states many times to help escaped slaves find their way to the North.

1863

Tubman works to free 500 slaves that had gathered at rebel outposts. Most of the freed slaves join the Union Army.

LOOK, LOOK AGAIN

Take a close look at this illustration of the Underground Railroad and answer the following questions:

1. How would an escaped slave describe this scene? What would a fugitive slave trying to make his or her way to safety think when looking at this scene?

2. What would a plantation owner see in this picture? What would he think of the fugitive slaves making their way toward freedom? What would he want to do? Why?

3. How would a man running for his life view this scene? How would he feel about the life he had to leave behind? How would he feel to be separated from his family?

GLOSSARY

abolish *(ah-BALL-ish)* to formally bring an end to something

bondage *(bon-DIJ)* the state of being enslaved

chattel *(CHAH-tell)* something that belongs to somebody; property that is not a house or a building

coopers *(KOO-purrs)* people who are skilled in making or repairing barrels

deficiency *(dee-FISH-en-see)* a lack of something

elude *(ee-LOOD)* to escape from danger or from a pursuer

free state *(FREE STAYT)* before the Civil War, a state of the United States in which slavery was not allowed

infractions *(in-FRACK-shuns)* violations of the law or a set of rules

masons *(MAY-suns)* people who are skilled in working with stone

rebellion *(ree-BELL-yun)* resisting authority

textile *(TECKS-tyle)* cloth or fabric

torture *(TOR-chur)* to mistreat or abuse

LEARN MORE

FURTHER READING

Bader, Bonnie. *The Underground Railroad.* New York: Scholastic, 2018.

Lassieur, Allison. *The Underground Railroad: An Interactive History Adventure.* Mankato, MN: Capstone Press, 2016.

Petry, Ann. *Harriet Tubman: Conductor on the Underground Railroad.* New York: Amistad, 2018.

WEBSITES

Enabling Freedom

http://freedomcenter.org/enabling-freedom/history

This website explains the history of the Underground Railroad and how it helped people make their way to freedom.

The Underground Railroad

http://www.pbs.org/wgbh/aia/part4/4p2944.html

This website describes the history and organization of the Underground Railroad.

INDEX

ABOUT THE AUTHOR

Kristin J. Russo is a university English lecturer. She loves teaching, reading, writing, and learning new things. She and her husband live near Providence, Rhode Island, in a small house surrounded by flower gardens. They have three grown children and three rescue dogs.